THE NINE FLORA McFLIMSEY BOOKS

Miss Flora McFlimsey and the Baby New Year

Miss Flora McFlimsey's Birthday

Miss Flora McFlimsey's Christmas Eve

Miss Flora McFlimsey's Easter Bonnet

Miss Flora McFlimsey's Halloween

Miss Flora McFlimsey and Little Laughing Water

Miss Flora McFlimsey and the Little Red Schoolhouse

Miss Flora McFlimsey's May Day

Miss Flora McFlimsey's Valentine

Miss Flora McFlimsey's May Day

BY MARIANA

Lothrop, Lee & Shepard Books   *New York*

ILLUSTRATIONS BY MARIANA RECREATED BY CAROLINE WALTON HOWE.

Copyright © 1969 by Mariana Foster Curtiss, 1987 by Erik Bjork.

First Edition   1 2 3 4 5 6 7 8 9 10

Library of Congress Cataloging in Publication Data
Mariana.   Miss Flora McFlimsey's May Day.
Summary: Although Miss McFlimsey knows she isn't beautiful, she discovers she has the potential for another queenly attribute.
[1. May Day—Fiction. 2. Dolls—Fiction. 3. Animals—Fiction] I. Title. PZ7.M33825M1 1987 [E] 86-15252
ISBN 0-688-04545-6   ISBN 0-688-04546-4 (lib. bdg.)

"Miss Flora McFlimsey, you're a perfect sight!" said the little girl. "Your face is dirty, and your hair hasn't been brushed for a week. It's May Day, too. But the way you look, *you'd* never be Queen of the May!"

She filled a bowl with warm water and found a tiny washcloth. Then she picked up Miss Flora McFlimsey, scrubbed her face, and brushed her hair and tied it back with her little black ribbon.

Just then the little girl's mother called her. She put Miss Flora McFlimsey back in her red rocking chair, gave her a kiss, and hurried out of the dollhouse.

Miss Flora McFlimsey sat quite still for a while. She was trying not to cry. "Nobody likes me," she thought.

She got up and went over and looked at herself in the mirror.

"I wish I were pretty," she whispered. "I wish I had long legs and curly hair and some eyebrows. My cheeks aren't very pink, and I don't care much for my nose either."

"Too bad you haven't got whiskers," remarked Pookoo, who was lying on the window seat. "There's nothing like whiskers to improve one's appearance. But pretty is as pretty does, Miss McFlimsey. Take me for example— there's not a better-behaved or handsomer cat in the neighborhood." He sat up and began to brush his whiskers.

Well, there wasn't much use
expecting sympathy from Pookoo.

Miss Flora McFlimsey put on her
straw hat and white gloves, and stuffed
a handkerchief in her apron pocket.
Then she went out to take a walk.

Everything was shining and beautiful in the morning light. The dewdrops sparkled like diamonds on the grass.

A little bird flew down and lit on her shoulder.

"Good morning, Miss Flora McFlimsey," he chirped. "Are you looking for worms?" And he began to sing—

"Tis the Merry Month of May!

All the world is green and gay."

But Miss Flora McFlimsey didn't feel in the least merry or gay, so she didn't answer, and soon the little bird flew away.

She started on the path that led into
the woods. She hadn't gone far before
there was a rustle in the bushes and out
hopped Peterkins.

"Goodbye, Miss Flora McFlimsey," he said. "Where are you going?"

Peterkins was a rather muddleheaded little rabbit who always got things mixed up. He said goodbye when he meant hello, and hello when he meant goodbye.

"I—I—don't know," answered Miss Flora McFlimsey.

"Well," said Peterkins, "*I* always know where *I'm* going. Sometimes I'm going nowhere, and sometimes I'm not going anywhere."

He came closer to Miss Flora McFlimsey and wiggled his ears excitedly. "But today I'm going *somewhere*! So, hello!" he cried and hopped off into the bushes.

Slowly Miss Flora McFlimsey walked on into the woods. A nut fell on her hat. Just over her head Miss Friskie Squirrel was sitting on a branch.

"Good morning, Miss McFlimsey," she called. "Sorry I can't come down and chatter with you, but I'm getting ready for the May Day party." She scampered higher up the tree.

"No one has invited *me* to a party," thought Miss Flora McFlimsey as she trudged on.

She felt very lonely. When she came to a big log lying across the path, she climbed up on top of it and sat down. She took out her pocket handkerchief and began to cry.

"Who's that walking on the top of my house?" said a squeaky voice. A queer little face was looking out at her from the end of the log.

"Oh," said Miss Flora McFlimsey, "I didn't know anyone lived here."

"I'm Mrs. Porcupine," said the
strange-looking creature, crawling up
beside her. "Porky to my friends."

Just then there came squeaks and squeals from inside the log.

"It's the children," exclaimed Mrs. Porcupine. "They always misbehave when they are left alone. They fight and throw things at one another. Today I must leave them and hunt for food. If only there were someone to stay with them!" And she began to cry.

Miss Flora McFlimsey handed her the pocket handkerchief.

"Don't cry," she said. "I'll stay with your children."

"Oh, that's very kind of you," said Mrs. Porcupine.

At that moment, out of the log
came three little objects that looked like
three pincushions stuck full of pins.

"This is Katy and Cavy and Ogilvie," said their mother. "I
do hope they won't give you any trouble. If they do," she
whispered, "just spank them."

Miss Flora McFlimsey looked at the little porcupines' sharp
quills and wondered just how that could be done.

"And now," said Mrs. Porcupine, "I'm off." And she
disappeared into the bushes.

Katy and Cavy and Ogilvie at once began throwing sticks and pebbles at one another.

"Let's dance," said Miss Flora McFlimsey.

They took paws and danced round and round until they all flopped down on the ground. But they were up again in a moment, squealing, "What'llwedo — What'llwedonow?"

"Let's play Tag," said Miss Flora McFlimsey.

The little porcupines responded with shrieks and whoops of delight, their quills standing straight up.

"Oh, oh, oh, oh, oh!" cried Miss
Flora McFlimsey. Her dress was torn,
her arms were scratched, and a quill was
sticking in her hat.

Just then Mrs. Porcupine's little black nose appeared from out of the bushes. At once Katy and Cavy and Ogilvie curled up into three small balls and lay quite still.

"I knew they'd be good," said their mother, beaming at them approvingly, "if only someone stayed with them."

She put down her bag of nuts and roots and shook hands with Miss Flora McFlimsey.

"It was most kind of you," she said. "Do drop in to the log anytime."

"Goodbye," squealed the little
porcupines, waving their paws.

Miss Flora McFlimsey waved back.
She was beginning to feel happy again.

She hadn't gone far before she heard someone crying. The sound seemed to come from a thicket in the woods.

Miss Flora McFlimsey ran over and tried to peer inside. A sign said: MRS. COTTONTAIL, HATS. But there seemed to be no entrance.

"Take four hops to the right," said a voice, "and three to the left, and you'll find the door."

Miss Flora McFlimsey jumped four times to her right and three to her left. She pushed the briars aside and there, sure enough, was a little door. She knocked.

"Come in," said the voice.

Miss Flora McFlimsey took off her hat and managed to squeeze through the door. Inside was a tiny room.

All around, hanging on the walls, were little hats—hats
made out of corn shucks, hats of birch bark, hats of straw,
hats trimmed with feathers and berries and robins' eggs.

Seated in the middle was an elderly rabbit. It was Peterkins'
aunt, Mrs. Cottontail.

Miss Flora McFlimsey remembered that Mrs. Cottontail had once sent her a lovely Easter bonnet.

"Peterkins promised to help," Mrs. Cottontail was murmuring, "but he's off—goodness knows where. Today of all days! And that Miss Squirrel promised, too. Never trust a squirrel—they're up a tree before you know it."

She began to cry.

Miss Flora McFlimsey hastily handed her the pocket handkerchief.

"What I need is flowers," explained Mrs. Cottontail, drying her eyes. "They are for a special occasion."

"Don't cry. I'll pick flowers for you," said Miss Flora McFlimsey.

And before Mrs. Cottontail could answer, Miss Flora McFlimsey had squeezed herself out of the door.

All around, violets were growing, and little white crocuses and bluebells and dandelions were peeping up among the leaves.

Three times Miss Flora McFlimsey
filled her apron with flowers and carried
them back to Mrs. Cottontail.
Then she helped her sort them out
and tie them together in little bunches.

The afternoon had almost gone before she remembered that Pookoo would soon be wanting his saucer of milk.

Mrs. Cottontail rubbed some rabbit ointment on Miss Flora McFlimsey's arms and mended her dress and gave her a hug.

Miss Flora McFlimsey was feeling very happy now. She couldn't find the path back to the dollhouse, but far off she heard music—so she followed the music until she came to the edge of the meadow.

She hid behind a tree and peeped out.

In the middle of the meadow was a Maypole. Peterkins and Pookoo and Oliver Owl and Miss Squirrel and Tuffy Puffin and Timothy Mouse were all there. They were dancing to the tune of the fiddle played by Cadmium Yellow, a friend of Pookoo. And they were calling, "Miss Flora McFlimsey. Miss Flora McFlimsey."

They carried her over and sat her on a throne made of flowers beneath the Maypole.

All at once Peterkins dashed off into the bushes. He was soon back wearing the hat that Miss Flora McFlimsey had left at Mrs. Cottontail's house. In his hand he carried a little crown of flowers. "This crown is from my aunt," he exclaimed. "It's for the Queen of the May. I—I—just forgot it. I mean I just remembered it."

They put the crown on Miss Flora McFlimsey's head while
the little bird on top of the Maypole sang—
"Tis the Merry Month of May!
All the world is green and gay."

The shadows were growing longer when Cadmium Yellow put down his fiddle, and the little bird on top of the Maypole flew away, and Pookoo and Miss Flora McFlimsey started back to the dollhouse.

"You're looking very well this evening, Miss McFlimsey," said Pookoo. "But handsome is as handsome does. Take me, for example—"

But Miss Flora McFlimsey wasn't listening. She was thinking what a happy day it had been.

Just before she got into bed she crept over and looked at herself in the mirror.

Maybe it was the moonlight—but her eyes were shining and her cheeks were pink. She thought she looked—well—almost pretty.

Then she climbed into bed and went peacefully to sleep.

```
JP                    97001122
Mariana
Miss Flora McFlimsey's May Day
```

OLD CHARLES TOWN LIBRARY
CHARLES TOWN, WV 25414